Bobby Normal
And The
Black Dragon

A.S.Chambers

This story is a work of fiction.
All names, characters and incidents portrayed are fictitious and the works of the author's imagination. Any resemblance to actual persons, living or dead is entirely coincidental.

This edition published in 2024.
Copyright © 2024 Basilisk Books.

All rights reserved. No part of this publication may be reproduced, stored in a retrieval system, or transmitted, in any form or by any means without the prior written permission of the publisher, nor be otherwise circulated in any form of binding or cover other than that in which it is published and without a similar condition being imposed on the subsequent purchaser.

A.S.Chambers asserts his moral right to be identified as the author of this work.

Cover art © 2024 Liam Shaw.

ISBN: 978-1-915679-24-6

Dedication

A huge thank you to everyone who kindly backed my Kickstarter campaign for this book. Special mentions go to
Charlie
Rebecca Armstrong
Simon Brindley
Ron Chick
Nadine Shinfield
Debs the SteamGoth
Bec Pearce
Francesco Tehrani
Paul
Miss Frog
Lee Hardy

Also, special thanks to the members of my Patreon Book Club for their valued support:
Kevin Denwood,
Jacob Matts,
Paul Lewis,
Gemma Innes.

For more details about my Book Club and how you can receive signed copies of my books when they are published, please visit my website:
www.aschambers.co.uk.

Also a huge thank you, once again, to Liam Shaw for his amazing cover art.

Also By A.S.Chambers

Sam Spallucci Series.
The Casebook of Sam Spallucci - 2012
Sam Spallucci: Ghosts From The Past - 2014
Sam Spallucci: Shadows of Lancaster – 2016
Sam Spallucci: The Case of The Belligerent Bard - 2016
Sam Spallucci: Dark Justice – 2018
Sam Spallucci: Troubled Souls - 2020
Sam Spallucci: Bloodline - Prologues & Epilogue – 2021
Sam Spallucci: Bloodline – 2021
Sam Spallucci: Fury of the Fallen - 2022
Sam Spallucci: The Case of The Pillaging Pirates - 2023
Sam Spallucci: Lux Æterna - Due 2024

Short Story Anthologies.
Oh Taste And See – 2014
All Things Dark And Dangerous – 2015
Let All Mortal Flesh – 2016
Mourning Has Broken – 2018
Hide Not Thou Thy Face – 2020
If Ye Loathe Me - 2022
Out of the Depths - 2023
Hear My Scare - Due 2025

Ebook short stories.
High Moon - 2013
Girls Just Wanna Have Fun – 2013
Needs Must - 2019

Novellas.
Songbird – 2019
Bobby Normal and The Eternal Talisman - 2021
Bobby Normal and the Virtuous Man - 2021
Bobby Normal and the Children of Cain - 2022
Bobby Normal and The Fallen - 2023
Child of Light - Due 2024
Child of Fire - Due 2025

Omnibuses.
Children of Cain - 2019
Macabre Collection: Volume One - 2022
Macabre Collection: Volume Two - 2023
Sam Spallucci Omnibus: Volume One - 2022
Sam Spallucci Omnibus: Volume Two - 2024
Bobby Normal - The Complete Adventures - 2024

CONTENTS

Previously...

Bobby is an orphan from the Divergent Lands, a desolate world in the far future, where humanity has been reduced to a pitiful remnant. Along with his hot-headed eight-year-old sister, Katy, he was entrusted to deliver the Eternal Talisman to a man named Jason who was residing in the neighbouring village. A priest, Jason was believed by some to be the prophesied Virtuous Man who was destined to overthrow the ruler of this grim land, Kanor, known by those who survived the genocide as the Black Dragon. However, Jason sent his troops on a disastrous mission in which everyone apart from the siblings was slaughtered by Kanor's golem foot soldiers — constructs. To make matters worse, Jason blamed

Bobby and Katy for the catastrophe, saying that they were secret servants of the Black Dragon himself.

The children were rescued by Claw, Tigress and Scorpion — three vampires that called themselves the Children of Cain. The supernatural creatures were searching for the man that Claw felt was the *true* Virtuous Man, his old friend Sam Spallucci. Tragically, Tigress and Scorpion died when the vampires and the orphans fought the fallen angel Asmodeus and his own band of construct soldiers. As the children tended to Claw's wounds, they were joined by an elderly man named Cutter. The old man had helped the two children numerous times on their adventures and they trusted him implicitly. However, the vampire Claw revealed that the siblings' ally was, in fact, a Shadow Wraith, an elite construct and a servant of Kanor.

Angry at the death of the two female vampires and the revelation regarding Cutter, Katy ran away. Bobby tracked her down before the female Fallen, Asherah, subsequently saved them both from a pack of wild dogs. Katy was impressed by the mysterious angel's powers so decided to leave Bobby and Claw in order to join her new saviour. Determined to rescue his sister, Bobby persuaded Claw to enlist the help of the reclusive Archangel Michael. Initially reluctant to get involved, Michael eventually accompanied the two friends to Sewell, Asherah's temple and stronghold. They successfully snatched the eight-year-old from the Fallen's insidious clutches.

However, Katy refused to remain with Bobby and Claw, demanding to be returned to Sewell, saying that it was somewhere that she felt she finally belonged. Bobby relented and returned his sister to Asherah before setting out on his own.

We join him as he arrives at a location that he has witnessed in his dreams. It is an old oak tree upon a barren hillside. Beneath it stands an individual who has visited him in his sleep — a being whose form continually shifts between that of a young girl, a middle-aged woman and an elderly crone. She informs Bobby that she wants him to save the one known as Sam Spallucci...

A.S.Chambers

Chapter One

Life, Bobby decided as he dismounted his horse and tethered it to a low-hanging branch from the voluminous oak tree, was indeed the most curious of things. Only a short while ago, his and Katy's entire existence had been centred around living on their wits, scavenging and stealing their next meal whilst avoiding the belligerent torments of the town bully, Teller.

The same Teller that Katy had pushed to his death from a bridge in Orchester.

Bobby sighed and rested his tired head against the warm neck of the chestnut brown steed. Taking a deep breath, he stood up straight, swallowed and, ignoring the curiously shapeshifting humanoid entity that was standing close by, wandered over to the vast tree. He allowed his fingers to trace the swirls and knots of the oak's rough bark. The patterned surface looked to him like a raging sea. Not that Bobby had ever *seen* a sea before. His father had just told him tales of people in the distant past venturing out on the vast watery expanses in search of new lands and undertaking great adventures. In the days before the rise of the Black Dragon, Kanor. In the days before the Divergence.

"My father would have loved this," the teenage boy murmured to himself.

"I am sure…" began the girl.

"…that he would have fashioned a great many items of furniture from its wood," finished the woman.

Bobby turned and faced the old crone. "You knew my father?"

"I know everything," stated the haggard old being.

Bobby leaned against the oak tree, crossed his arms across his chest and frowned as he studied the curious figure before him. Right now, he was not in the mood for mysterious riddles or insinuations. With

Katy's departure and the revelation that Cutter was a Shadow Wraith, his world had been torn apart and thrown in front of a raging hog. Right now he could feel the heavy trotters pounding up and down upon his tired spine. His tongue was writhing behind his teeth, wanting desperately to spit words of anger at his latest tormentor.

However, the mention of his dead father brought back the memory of the brown-haired, gentle-faced man and a certain cantankerous customer. An elderly resident of Irlingbury had requested that Howard build him a fence to surround his small property. The old man had said that it was to stop children from strolling aimlessly across his vegetable patch, destroying his small crop of produce. Bobby's father had agreed to take on the job and produced a fence that had been fashioned from small branches and twigs from the scant supply of wood that he had scavenged outside the village. However, the customer had been less than impressed. He cried that if he had wanted a fence made from scraps then he would have simply scattered tatty bits of firewood around the boundary of his property. Howard politely explained that this was currently all the wood available for such a task as Kanor's troops had only recently levelled the woodlands nearby. There simply was not any wood of a larger nature. The old man had not backed down and had screamed that Howard was a charlatan and a fraud. He had marched off into his house and had slammed the door behind him.

Howard had simply nodded to himself, gathered up the fencing material, placed it on his handcart and trundled it back to his cottage.

Not once did he protest. Not once did he raise his own voice in anger.

Bobby had been amazed at his father's calm reaction and asked him why he had not demanded that the customer pay him for his work with the agreed goods.

"My son, we never really know what's going on in someone's life. We only ever see glimpses, fleeting images that are part of a complicated story. As a result, we should never, ever judge someone by their actions alone until we fully understand what has driven them to behave in what we might, ourselves, consider to be an unpleasant manner. Just a few weeks ago, that man's wife of many years succumbed to a fever. Their garden was her pride and joy. She would spend hour upon hour in it whilst she tended to her vegetables and flowers. She was a very common sight for all passersby. Now that she is dead, she is already fading from the memory of those who knew her. Indeed, the children of the village, who care not for the production of food and flora, just see the garden as a shortcut across the corner between two streets.

"Our friend there, mind, sees the actions of the children as an affront to the memory of his loved one. Naturally, he wants to preserve the garden as it was so that he can cling to that memory in his own final years. It is only natural that he should want to do so in what he would see as the most fitting manner possible. So, my guess is that when he came up with the idea of a fence, he imagined a much grander affair that was fashioned from nice smooth planks of timber rather than these pitiful remnants that I was able to acquire. I could have argued until I was blue in the face that there was currently no such timber available for his fence due to the actions of Kanor's troops, but it would have been to no avail. He would never have listened; never seen reason.

"Grief can do terrible things to folk. All we can do is nod, smile, wish them to walk well and stay safe whilst guarding our own tongue and prevent the matter at hand from becoming far worse than it already is."

Bobby continued to lean against the old tree and guarded his tongue.

The girl smiled. "Your father taught you well."

Bobby remained cautiously silent. Rather than replying, he studied the threefold being. Quite obviously not human, its eyes were pools of pure water. A deep blue, they swirled and flowed around their sockets making it quite impossible to figure out exactly what they were looking at. Her hair was grey and swept down over her shoulders as if it were a river in full flood. The creature was attired in what appeared to be a long dress fashioned from some sort of flowing liquid in which there were flashes of fire.

"That is why I feel you are suited to my task," continued the woman as her unsettling eyes regarded Bobby.

"But first," finished the crone, "you have questions. Two in fact."

The boy nodded. "Obvious one first, then. Who are you?"

"I," proclaimed the girl, "am the sea that flows between the three Realms of Heaven, Beyond and the Physical Realm. From the beginning of time, I have kept all three in check, ensuring that there is order in what would otherwise be chaos. The eternal song of creation sails upon my mighty currents, crying out to all who would lift their ears in order to listen. I am the Abyss."

Bobby nodded. "I've heard about the Realms before."

"From the Children of Cain," said the woman.

"I showed you to them," said the crone, "when they first met me."

This revelation pierced Bobby's armour

of calm. He pulled away from the large tree. "They didn't mention that."

"It is of no concern," shrugged the girl. "It was a long time ago and much has happened since then."

"They were younger," explained the woman, "and were somewhat... preoccupied."

Bobby shuddered. He closed and re-opened his eyes. "Show me," he demanded. "Show me what you really are."

The crone nodded and all around them changed. Bobby was no longer standing upon a hillside in the Divergent Lands. Instead, he found himself suspended in complete darkness. For a moment, blind panic overtook him and he screamed helplessly into a void that swallowed all sound.

All sound except for one.

Out of the darkness came a voice that was impossible to describe.

"... ... ..."

It reached his ears as a threefold rhythm and it beat an enticing melody against his tympani that sang of beauty, of hope, of creation. Then, in the darkness there was Light.

An explosion burst from a distant point and the void was filled with song. The song coalesced and flowed as a mighty ocean. As its waters boiled with fire, it split the darkness in two. On one side was a place infused with light; on the other was a place of blackness. Then the song rose in volume and intensity and a third place formed, split from the other two. This was a place of vibrancy, of life. All three Realms coexisted in harmony with the mighty Abyss surging between them, keeping them apart and separate.

And, all the time, the threefold rhythm crashed upon the shores of the three Realms. As it did so, Bobby could now hear words attached to the rhythm:

We are one...

We are one...

We are one...

But there was more. Even through the immensity of the universe's might and grandeur, Bobby could sense more.

Would you see it? came a soft voice in his head.

"Show me," the boy replied.

Beyond the three Realms, a fire erupted into the surrounding darkness. Bobby watched as it expanded in size and illumination. A six-winged figure rose above all that existed. In its hands, it held a chalice and a sword. Its lips moved in time to the threefold song as it swung the sword and all creation cascaded down into the bowl of the chalice until there was nothing apart from a small, solitary ember.

Bobby gasped and crashed to the dew-soaked floor under the great oak tree. He looked up at the shifting form of the ocean that kept the universe in check.

"The Eternals," explained the girl. "When they sing their song as one, all will be destroyed."

"When?" Bobby managed.

"It has happened," said the woman.

"It will come to pass," explained the crone.

"Everything?"

The Abyss nodded: girl, woman, crone.

"How can I stop it?"

"That is the wrong question."

Bobby nodded. "Who is Sam Spal-lucci?"

A small fire cracked and popped as the day grew late. Embers floated up into the air, accompanied by frenetic sparks from the burning bracken and scavenged fragments of wood. Bobby held his hands out to the flames, warming them against the growing chill.

The soothing heat reached his skin but not his insides.

What the Abyss had shown him had chilled him to the core.

Everything swept away.

Absolutely everything.

No Earth, no Divergent Lands, no constructs, no Kanor.

Some might say that was a good thing. They would say that it was an end to this brutal cycle of destruction brought about by the Black Dragon. They would point out that the world, as it stood, was a rabid dog in agony as poisonous insanity consumed its brain; that it would finally be at peace as its owner cracked its skull open with a heavy rock. Let the being rise that would destroy everything! Let it bring an end to the carnage and chaos! There would be peace once more. Humanity had been given a chance and had failed. It had birthed Kanor from its loins, allowing the Black Dragon to spread his obsidian wings and decimate its hapless parent to a pitiful remnant.

But not Bobby.

As the teenage boy watched the fire dancing in the growing twilight, he knew that there had to be a way to prevent the devast-ation. Not just in his gut; not just some in-stinct. The Abyss had told him so.

What's more, there was a bonus.

"Sam Spallucci is a pivotal character in the history of humanity," the girl had said.

"If you save him…" continued the wo-man.

"…then Kanor will not rise," finished the crone.

A piece of wood collapsed in on itself and a plume of embers spiralled into the air as the fire changed shape. One small action had altered the structure of the hearth.

One small change in history could prevent the rise of Kanor. Prevent the Divergence from ever happening.

Bobby let that possibility hang suspended in his mind. What would that actually mean? If he went back and prevented the rise of the Black Dragon, what would that actually do? Everything would be different. Absolutely everything. No constructs, no poverty, no pain.

But what else would not exist?

He himself was a child of the Divergent Lands. If they did not come to pass, then how could he go back to prevent them?

The Abyss had added a new word to his vocabulary: paradox.

"You will be a thing out of time," explained the girl.

"A thing that should not exist yet does," said the woman.

"You would not be the first of these things as they have happened before," continued the crone.

Bobby sighed. Yes, life truly was far more complex than it used to be.

"What about Katy?" he had asked the shifting persona of the ocean that encompassed reality. "What about all the other people that have existed since the Divergence? Surely, if I prevent the rise of Kanor, then they will cease to exist."

"Do you think they enjoy their existence?" asked the girl. She waved a hand across the air in front of her and an apparition appeared. It showed a cohort of constructs marching through a small village putting to the lance all those who stood in their way.

"If you prevent the Divergence, you will prevent all this pain," stated the woman, her watery eyes holding fast onto the boy.

Bobby shook his head. "But life is far more than that. There is love here in this world as well as pain. Mothers give birth to babies who are cradled in the arms of their fathers. There is still beauty. You just have to look for it."

"But there is suffering too," said the crone. "You need look no further than the end of your nose in order to see the pain that this world endures."

"Why me? Why should I be the one to bring about change?"

"Because I know you will. I have already seen it."

So, as surely as the sun rose in the sky each morning, Bobby's destiny was already laid out in front of him. According to the Abyss, he had no choice.

According to the Abyss…

"No," he had said. "I can't do it. I won't. This may be a terrible place, but it can change. Humanity is resilient. It has existed this long, even under the crushing yoke of Kanor, so it can continue to survive and then, someday, it will rise up once more and overthrow him. He is called the Black Dragon, but he is just a man and men die. Kanor will perish one day. It may be in my lifetime; it may be in the future. But he will die, just as all men do. Then, on that day, humanity will be reborn.

"It doesn't need me to go back and erase all that has happened since the day of the Divergence. That would make me no better than that being you showed me erad-icating all the universe. I do not have the right to alter what has gone before."

Then the Abyss had done something

truly unsettling. The girl, the woman and the crone had all smiled. "You say that now," they said, "but you will change your mind. When you do, you will travel to the church in Wellington, to the lair of Kanor himself. There you will lay your hand upon the font, the stone basin at the back of the church and I will transport you back to a time before all of this. I will take you back to a world before the Black Dragon rose and scorched the land and I will deposit you in a city called Lancaster.

"There you *will* find Sam Spallucci."

Then, without saying another word, the manifestation of the Abyss had simply vanished, leaving Bobby standing on the barren hillside under the old oak tree. Cursing under his breath, he had climbed up onto his horse and ridden as far away from that spot as he could before the night had begun to creep upon him.

So here he was sitting in front of a small fire with sleep tugging at his eyes as the soothing warmth reached out to him. Here he was, adamant that he would defy an entity that had mastery over time and claimed to know his fate.

Here he was, drawing a line in the dirt and saying that he would not cross over. Contrary to what the Abyss claimed, he was the master of his own destiny.

And, with that, Bobby allowed his eyes to shut and he drifted off to sleep.

A.S.Chambers

Chapter Two

Bobby did not sleep well. As he lay on the ground in front of the dwindling fire, his mind was not filled with images of a being wiping a universal slate clean or of the Black Dragon rising into the air, scorching the ground below with his infernal breath. There weren't even any constructs marching into a grubby, defenceless settlement, subjecting all the villagers to brutal deaths.

There was none of this.

There was just Katy.

He was chasing his sister as she ran through a similar meadow of scarlet flowers to the one which he had seen in his previous dream. Bobby kept reaching out to grab her, to pull her back, but she was always just that bit too far ahead of his grasping fingers.

Not that she wanted to be caught.

His sister was laughing happily to herself as she ran her fingers through the small red blooms. As she did so, her hands came away stained with their colour. Rather than disturbing her, this caused Katy to laugh even more. "Look, Bobby! Look!" she cried with glee over her shoulder, lifting her hands above her head for him to see.

As Bobby watched, the red pigment on his sibling's fingers began to drip down onto her head. The two children stopped and Katy lifted her face to her hands. Opening her mouth she let a drop of the liquid fall upon her tongue. "Yes!" she cried. "Yes!" and she thrust her hands into her mouth, devouring all that she could of the viscous substance.

Bobby reached out again, but still he could not grab his sister, even though they were both standing still. She seemed to be drawing even further away. The boy frowned at the impossibility of the situation then gasped as his sister aged. Now she stood in front of him in what looked to be her early twenties. Her now pallid skin contrasted against the black cloak that she wore over her shoulders. "See what I am become..." she hissed.

Bobby's nose twitched as the familiar smell of burning reached him and, behind the older Katy, the horizon erupted into flame. A wicked grin formed on her mouth and a pair of sharp fangs were all too clear to see at the edges of her red lips.

"See what I am become..." she repeated as she turned and sprinted towards the flames, drawing a sword as she did so.

Bobby screamed silently after her and tried to follow, but he kept stumbling. Looking down, he saw that his path was strewn with corpses, all bearing agonised death masks. Again he cried out and again his voice was silent.

Katy turned to face her impotent brother. This time she had a boy of Bobby's age clasped in her arms. The teenager was terrified and was screaming for his life.

"See what you let me become..." Katy growled as she thrust her face into the unfortunate lad's neck and ripped at his skin with her sharp fangs. Moaning joyfully, Katy drank deeply from the ravaged skin as the boy finally fell limp and she threw him, discarded and empty, with the other corpses. "You could have stopped this, but you didn't," she declared. "You let me become this." And in a motion that was faster than Bobby could comprehend, Katy was nose to nose with him, the blood of the dead boy covering her face and assaulting her brother's senses.

Bobby awoke with a shout and with an overwhelming sense of confusion.

The nightmare was not the only cause of this abrupt awakening.

The pricking sensation of a clay lance at his throat was also a contributing factor.

Bobby silently cursed his idiocy as his horse jolted underneath him. His hands were bound in front of him, the cords digging into his wrists as a reminder that one must never let down one's guard in the Divergent Lands. His encounter with the Abyss had caused him to be distracted and it had cost him his freedom.

He considered himself fortunate that it

had not cost him his life.

His mount was tethered to that of a Shadow Wraith that rode in front of him. Another rode behind and the three horses were flanked with numerous constructs that marched in their ubiquitous precision.

Thud… thud…

Thud… thud…

Thud… thud…

As soon as he had awoken, Bobby had realised that trying to run would have been pointless. Not only had one construct been holding a lance to his throat but he had been surrounded, as he was now, by a full cohort.

"You will come with us," one of the Wraiths had instructed and that had been all. Nothing else. No threats, no explanations. They had simply motioned that he should mount his horse, to the saddle of which he had then been bound, and they had set off away from where he had spent his dream-filled night.

Something was going on and Bobby had no idea as to what. On the plus side, he was still breathing, so he took that as a win and decided to wait and see what would happen next.

He didn't have to wait too long. After half a day's ride, they arrived at an enormous building that rose out of a flat plain. Human guards stood at the gateway and stamped to attention as the party rode through into a large courtyard. The lead Shadow Wraith leapt gracefully from its steed and pointed to Bobby. A construct turned and whipped out an extended arm like a lasso. It snaked its limb around the boy and lifted him effortlessly from his saddle before depositing him on the cobbled floor.

"Thank you," Bobby smiled politely.

The construct, needless to say, did not reply. Instead, it turned, fell into step with the rest of its cohort and marched off into the complex.

Bobby shrugged, faced the two Wraiths and raised a questioning eyebrow.

"Come with us," one of them replied before shoving Bobby towards a large pair of wooden doors at the edge of the courtyard.

As he approached the doors, Bobby paused and gazed up in wonder. Never had he seen doors of such a size. The amount of timber required to manufacture them would have been immense. No mean feat in a land where Kanor's forces systematically slashed and burned the woodland. Whoever owned this fortress was certainly a person of great power and obscene wealth.

He had only ever seen one such building before. The temple of Asherah. Which probably meant…

As the massive doors swung solidly shut behind him, Bobby's suspicions were confirmed. He found himself standing in a long room with a golden throne at the opposite end of a long, red carpet. Dotted along the edge of the carpet, and leading up to the majestic seat of power, were numerous statues. They all showed the same man in what Bobby took to be heroic poses of some sort. There he was fighting a man with a head resembling that of a bull. There he was decapitating a crazy figure of a woman with snakes in her hair. There he was standing proudly on a boat with other men in unrecognisable clothing. There he was… Bobby frowned. The statue of the man seemed to have some sort of contraption over its head and its clothing was large and bulky. It seemed to be stepping down a small ladder from a weird little house on legs onto a very bumpy surface.

Each to their own: he thought as he walked past the statuary and up to the throne upon which was seated an individual whom he had last encountered on a battlefield.

"Kneel before Lord Asmodeus," growled the Wraith. Bobby felt a rough shove between his shoulder blades and he collapsed onto his knees.

The male Fallen waved a hand of dismissal at the two Shadow Wraiths and they departed in silence. He was lounging nonchalantly with one leg over an arm of the golden throne and was attired in long blue robes that curled around his arms and legs. "So, *Bobby Normal* (I believe that's your name), what do you make of my grand palace? I bet you've never seen something so fine before, have you?"

Bobby was tempted for just a brief moment to say that he had preferred the temple of Asherah but, before his mouth snapped the words out, he caught sight of the two thunderbolts on the top of the throne and decided better of it. "It's truly unique," he said, "and completely beyond my comprehension."

Asmodeus seemed to consider the reply as electricity flickered absentmindedly across his knuckles. He nodded and flicked a finger. Bobby flinched involuntarily as a shower of sparks flew across the air towards him. However, they landed on the bonds between his hands, burning them apart and setting his wrists free. "Thank you," he said, rubbing at his wrists.

"You see, Bobby, I can be quite magnanimous when I want to be," drawled the fallen angel, idly watching more electricity dancing across his fingertips. "I find it can be quite useful." He paused and lifted the index finger on his right hand. A spark of electricity grew in size just above his fingertip.

Bobby swallowed.

Asmodeus ignored the boy's growing discomfort and just appeared to study the dancing electricity as it continued to grow in size. "So, let's get straight to the point, shall we? My *employer*," Bobby could not help but notice the disdain in the word, "appears to be somewhat fascinated with you. Back at Rishton, I could have fried you to a crisp, but there would have been dire consequences." He finally shot a glance at the kneeling prisoner. "And not just for you." Repositioning himself so that Bobby became his entire field of vision, Asmodeus leaned forward, the spark of electricity on his finger directly between him and the human. "Tell me, why is Kanor obsessed with a street urchin?"

This was not good. Bobby stared at the dancing spark of energy and wracked his brain for an answer. The wrong one could lead to agonising repercussions.

"I don't know," he answered honestly then shot his hands out in front of him as Asmodeus made to flick his wrist. "Wait! I truly don't know. I am a nobody! Normal, like you said. Yet I seem to have been dragged into this incredible world of yours. I don't know why. It perplexes me, confounds me and baffles me. Why should the decimator of humanity be obsessed with a teenage boy from a small village in the middle of nowhere?" He paused, considered his next words very carefully and then continued: "I am sure that an esteemed Lord like yourself has far more insight into the matter than a lowly individual such as me."

Bobby closed his eyes and awaited the agonising surge of electricity.

It never came.

Opening his eyes, he watched Asmodeus palm the spark and then frown momentarily before allowing a smile to spread across his face. "That does make sense," he nodded. "If I cannot comprehend the mind of my *master*," there was the animosity once again, "then how can I expect you, a mere human, to do so?"

Bobby decided that now would be a good time to perform a bit of prying, whilst the Fallen was enjoying having his ego stroked. "If I may, my Lord? It appears to me that you do not enjoy having your angelic self pushed around by the Black Dragon."

Asmodeus slouched back on his throne, a sullen look on his face. "You may be just a human, Normal, but you seem to be quite perceptive. My relationship with the Black Dragon is… *complicated.*"

"How so?"

The Fallen opened his mouth to speak but there was a commotion and the doors were thrown open as a Shadow Wraith entered. "Apologies, my Lord," it called across the room, "but it is urgent."

Asmodeus beckoned for him to approach the throne.

"We have located them."

The angel raised an eyebrow. "Really? Well, that *is* good news. Where?"

"Those who defied you are a day's march north of here. We can muster a cohort and be upon them before sunset tomorrow."

Asmodeus clapped his hands with glee and a shower of sparking electricity plumed from between his palms. "Excellent. We shall hunt them down, pounce when they're not expecting it and ram their heads upon poles in the torched remains of their village. No others would dare to defy me when they see the consequences of their futile actions." He rose from the throne. "Normal, our little chat will have to be put on hold." To the Wraith: "Have him taken to the dungeon. I'll ready my troops for the hunt." With that, he strode gleefully out of the throne room.

The Shadow Wraith turned to Bobby and grabbed him roughly by the shoulder.

As Bobby was not-so-gently escorted through the twisting corridors of Asmodeus' fortress, he knew that he should have felt sick to the pit of his stomach with worry and terror. The weird thing was that, instead of a blind panic coursing through his body, he was experiencing a peculiar sort of calm. As he passed numerous constructs marching through the passageways, he considered just how many times he had run into them out in the wide world. He couldn't quite put a number on it, but the encounters were certainly starting to rack up.

And he had survived every one.

Was it luck? Was it skill? Was it the ability to run crazily fast when being pursued by a murderous lump of clay on two legs? Perhaps it was a combination of all of the above?

Would it be the same this time?

Well, Bobby surmised, he wasn't dead yet. He had been captured and brought alive to the Fallen. Then, when in Asmodeus' presence, the angel hadn't even lain an electrically charged finger upon him. Bobby had the feeling that Asmodeus valued him more with a pulse than as a charred piece of meat.

What actually worried him though, as he was pushed into a small cell at the end of a dark passageway, was that this was the second time he had been told that the Black Dragon knew of him and was *obsessed* with him. Asherah had said exactly the same thing. This really did not sound good.

The bars clanged shut and Bobby turned to watch the Shadow Wraith stalk away, leaving two constructs standing motionless in front of the cell. The imprisoned teenager blew out a long breath, stretched and took in his new environment.

After no more than a few seconds, he decided that there wasn't really much to see. Stone walls, bucket, straw: that was all. With nothing else to occupy his interest, he turned his attention to his guards.

"So, do you do this a lot? Guarding, I mean. Must make a change to the stompy-stompy, stabby-stabby. Get a chance to rest and have some peace and quiet? Or, perhaps this is punishment duty? Did you do something wrong? Let someone go who you should have skewered? I can imagine your great leader has a bit of a temper when things don't go according to plan. We used to have someone like that back in Irlingbury. We had this crazy person who from time to time would just lose it. No one ever knew why. He just stormed around the streets every now and then, screaming and shouting at people. One time, he took his toilet bucket and threw it at a passerby. The look on her face! You really should have seen it." Bobby paused. "But, of course, you wouldn't have been able to, would you? Not having eyes. I guess you'd just have slipped your long tongue out and wriggled it around like you do, scenting the air." He shook his head. "The stench would have made even one of *you* cringe."

Bobby paused. The constructs hadn't

moved at all. Were they even listening?

He rested his head against one of the bars. "I don't normally talk to myself. I guess I'm just not used to being on my own. I have a sister, you see. She was always there with me. Normally eating or complaining, but always there. More often than not, she was the one who'd be filling the silences. She's younger than me, you see? So, she has a lot more unanswered questions bubbling around inside of her. That and..." In his head, Bobby watched Katy pushing Teller to his death. "That and something else..." He closed his eyes and just stood there with his head leaning on the bars to his cell.

The sound of footsteps broke his reverie and he straightened up, opening his eyes to see who was coming.

It was a Shadow Wraith.

Correction, it was a very familiar Shadow Wraith.

Bobby watched as Cutter marched down the corridor with absolute authority and presented himself before the two guards. "Our Lord demands that I take the prisoner to him right now."

The two constructs stepped aside, allowing Cutter access to the cell. The Wraith placed his hand over the locking mechanism and Bobby heard the wet sound of transformation as his "flesh" slipped into the metal workings. Cutter twisted his wrist and the door swung open. He withdrew his key-shaped hand, shook it, and his fingers slid back into position. "Come," he said to Bobby, gesticulating with the newly formed digits.

Cautiously, Bobby emerged from the cell, passing between the two guards. Cutter gestured for him to walk in front, which he did. When they had turned a couple of corners, the Shadow Wraith bent forward and whispered in his ear, "Stay close and do as I say."

"Why? So you can get me safely to your master?"

"No, Bobby. So I can get you out of here alive."

Bobby's heart leapt, but he kept his emotions in check and carried on walking. As they retraced his earlier journey, the boy and the Shadow Wraith passed numerous constructs, all of which stood to one side to let their superior pass. Not once were they challenged.

That was until they emerged into the courtyard of the fortress.

As soon as they stepped foot into the yard, Bobby's heart sank. It was far busier than it had been when he'd arrived. Now there were dozens of constructs swarming out of arches and doorways around the perimeter of the courtyard. They were all making their way to the central area where they were falling into line, forming an army.

In their midst was the same Shadow Wraith that had taken Bobby to Asmodeus. His head rose from his task at hand and his attention was diverted from organising the troops to the arrival of the two newcomers in the courtyard. Frowning, he marched over to Bobby and Cutter. "What's going on here? Where are you taking the prisoner?"

Bobby watched as six constructs peeled off from their formation and stamped over to behind their commander. This was not looking good.

"Well," Cutter began, "I could tell you

that Asmodeus has requested the presence of the boy, but then again, for what good that'll do me, I might as well tell you that the moon is made of cheese."

The commander frowned and made to speak, but his words were cut short as Cutter's left hand transformed into a lance and impaled the Wraith's face.

"Run for the gate!"

Bobby didn't need telling twice and he darted towards the main gate of the fortress. All around him, hell was breaking loose. He could hear Shadow Wraiths screaming commands, constructs stamping to action and human vassals presenting arms. One of the human guards jumped in front of him. Bobby kicked him squarely in the shins, causing the traitor to drop his pike and squeal in agony. Another grabbed Bobby by the arm but the boy dropped down into a roll, taking his would-be captor to the floor. As the teenager came back up to his feet, he stamped down angrily onto the man's face. Blood and cartilage erupted from the guard's nose.

The ground beside Bobby shook as a giant construct marched up towards him. He jinked left and right, making himself harder to target. However, his plan failed as he felt his feet swept out from beneath him. Cursing as he fell to the cobbled floor, he struggled onto his back and saw the construct's extended arm wrapped around his ankle. Bobby kicked with his free foot at the clay coil but the golem ignored the futile effort and relentlessly reeled him in.

There was a deafening roar from the melee in the courtyard and Bobby's attention was diverted from his impending fate. A knot of constructs was sent flying like twigs before a storm as a mass of fur and teeth burst from their midst. The simulacrum of a gigantic wolf bounded across the battlefield, throwing to one side any being that dared to block its path. In one final leap, it descended upon the extended arm of the construct and clamped down with its ferocious jaws. Bobby felt the coil around his leg slacken.

Cutter presented his back to the teenage boy. "Get on!" his gruff voice growled.

Bobby climbed aboard, clung on tight to the wiry hair and kept his head low, close to the powerful shoulders, as Cutter propelled the two of them out of the fortress and off to freedom.

43

Chapter Three

Cutter made sure that they were a safe distance from the fortress of Asmodeus before he allowed himself to slow down. His wolf form drew to a halt and he let Bobby dismount. When his passenger was securely on the ground, the wolf transformed into his usual shape of an old man dressed in ragged clothes.

"Are you okay?"

Bobby nodded, his eyes studying the grassy floor at his feet.

His rescuer sighed and walked over to a thicket of thorny bushes. Grumbling as he parted the treacherous branches, Cutter pulled out a long staff and a tatty-looking travelling bag. After slinging the bag over his shoulder, he rummaged in its depths until he found some dried fruit.

"Here. Eat this."

The teenager just stared at the offering.

"Bobby…"

"You think this makes everything okay?"

The old man's face filled with sorrow and regret. "Please. You need to eat."

"Why would I eat anything you offer me?"

"Because you look like you haven't had a square meal in days. What have you been doing?"

"It's none of your concern." With that, Bobby turned and began to walk away.

Cutter shoved the fruit back into his bag and trailed after the angry teenager. "You're just going to walk around while Asmodeus sends his goons out looking for you? That doesn't sound like a good idea."

"You have a better one?"

"Yes. Let me take you far away. Somewhere safe."

Bobby shook his head. "Well, what do you know? A cowardly construct. Who would have thought?"

"Right, that's enough of this swill." Cutter marched in front of the boy and thrust his staff defiantly onto the ground. "Out with it! Come on. Let's hear it!"

Bobby glared up at the old man. "What's there to say? You killed my father. You single-handedly tore my life apart! How in all the Divergent Lands can you possibly think I could ever forgive you for that? So, you burst in back there and sprung me from my cell. Thank you, kindly. Much appreciated. Now, go! Get out of my life! I don't need you anymore."

Bobby made to push past the old man, but Cutter's hand snapped out and grabbed him by the wrist.

"Let go!"

"No. Not until I've said my piece."

"What? That you had no choice? That you were made that way? Only following orders?"

"I could. But it would be pointless. Words mean nothing, Bobby. They are just fawning vanities that the guilty use to smooth rushing waters. Actions speak far louder. Judge me by my deeds. Weigh them as a baker weighs their grain. Look at what I've done and see if they balance out. I've been following you now since you left Irling-bury with Katy and Persephone. That was the first time that I intervened, when Teller was chasing you on the outskirts of the vil-lage."

Bobby frowned as he remembered the event, just before he, Katy and the girl en-trusted with the Eternal Talisman had es-caped down into the tunnels. "They thought they saw me down the street. That was you?"

Cutter nodded and there before Bobby was standing a simulacrum of himself.

"Well, that's weird."

His reflection nodded and shifted back into its previous form. "Constructs can look however they want. They can blend into a crowd and pass for humans. You could be walking along and have no knowledge that they are right next to you until the lance thrusts out of your dead heart. If you wander off on your own, Asmodeus *will* track you down. He will drag you back to his strong-hold and he will do whatever he desires to you.

"It won't be pretty."

"So, you think I should just run away and hide?"

"It is the sensible thing to do."

"But it's not the *right* thing."

Cutter crossed his arms. "What else do you have in mind then?"

"Something that might help you win back my trust."

They found the villagers who had defied Asmodeus shortly before the sun reached its zenith. Cutter had transformed into a sleek black stallion and they had galloped northwards, just as the Shadow Wraith had described, locating the rag-tag bunch of people encamped by a stream.

The boy and the horse looked down on them from a nearby hill.

"I think," Bobby said to his currently equine partner, that you ought to transform before we introduce ourselves. Don't want to terrify the people we're here to save."

The black horse nodded and shifted form. "About that. Just how do you intend to save a weary bunch of fugitives from an organised and vicious army of constructs."

Bobby gazed down into the valley below, mentally totting up the number of humans. There seemed to be about five dozen. "There's a good amount of them."

"But, even from here, you can see they are broken," Cutter protested, leaning heavily on his staff after he took it from Bobby. "You don't know what they've already been through, but knowing the forces of the Fallen, it will have been brutal and harrowing. They will have suffered and will have already seen loved ones fall to the lance."

"Then it's a good job I've got something that they've never possessed before."

"Please don't say *hope*," Cutter grumbled.

A smile touched Bobby's lips as he prodded Cutter's chest with a finger. "Oh no. Something far more useful than that. Someone who knows exactly how constructs think and how they can be outsmarted." With that, he headed down the hill to the refugees.

It quickly became all too apparent to Bobby that Cutter had been right about the fleeing villagers. They were disheartened, tired and scared to death.

As a result, the news that an army of constructs would be upon them by nightfall was not received very well.

"We must flee this place at once!" cried a stout man in a tunic that matched the redness in his jowly face. "Let's pack up and head north."

"We can't outrun them," protested another villager. "They will slaughter us." He slammed his face into his hands and began to weep.

Similar notions circulated around the crowd. About half began to pack up their meagre belongings whilst the rest simply sat down and awaited their fate.

"No! Wait!" Bobby cried. "Listen to me. There is another way."

Eyes brimming with fear turned towards the teenage boy.

"We can fight."

A woman pushed her way through the stunned group. "Are you insane? Have you not seen what fighting has already brought us?" She waved a hand at her companions. "Look at us. We have little enough energy left to walk let alone take on an army of mud buckets. Boy, you don't know what we've been through. You've not seen what they did to our loved ones. Who are you to tell us to fight?"

Bobby swallowed. He felt the unbearable weight of so many people staring at him. What he said now would affect their fate for good or ill. He knew he had to get it right.

"No, you're right. I don't know what you've already been through. You look to me like a bed sheet that has been wrung out after it has been washed; you hang heavy where you stand and are not what you used to be. You are defeated and broken. You are a shell of what I imagine you used to be. But, let me tell you this, neither running nor lying down to die will solve your problems.

"Because they're not just your own.

"They are the shared problems of all of us living in the hell forged by the Black Dragon. Look at yourselves. Your tiredness and your fear are not your greatest problems. The fact that you are divided in what you should do is what is preventing you from striking back. And that is what Kanor and his forces use as their greatest weapon: division.

"Think about it. How often did you socialise with people from other settlements? How often, when a trader came to your town did you eye him with suspicion? More often than not you were probably afraid that he was a quisling for one of the Fallen or, even worse, a construct in human form."

Some heads started to nod.

Bobby pressed on. "My home village was divided in the same way. A man named Teller was placed in charge of running things. He, his son and his cronies spied upon the rest of us and reported any misdeeds to higher powers. It was because of them that my father was put to the lance.

"And no one did anything about it.

"Instead, people went on with their lives as if nothing had happened."

"They murdered my daughter," snarled the woman.

"What was her name?"

The woman's eyes turned towards Cutter, who had asked the question.

"It was Anna. She was named after my younger sister, who died when I was but a teenager."

The old man nodded. "I'm sorry to hear that…?" He paused and allowed the woman to fill in the unasked question.

"Martha. My name is Martha." It was obvious to all that she was fighting back tears.

"Martha," continued Cutter, "what was the charge?"

"They accused her of plotting against Kanor. She was a child. Just a child! They dragged her screaming into the village square where a damned Wraith sliced her head off with a scythe he'd fashioned from his arm. We took them by surprise. It was only a small group, a Wraith and two of the mud buckets, and we were able to over-power them."

"What did you do?"

"Fire. We rained fire down upon them. With long poles, we harried them into an old barn and we torched them. We baked them solid then dragged their corpses out into the square where we ground them up and danced on their dust.

"But, someone must have betrayed us. An army came the next day. So many were killed. We had no choice but to run."

Cutter nodded. "You did what you had to do at that time."

"But now," Bobby said, "you can do something else. You can turn and fight. You can beat them back and, in doing so, send a message to the rest of the Divergent Lands that we can stand up for what we love, that we can beat them.

"We will be divided no more.

"We will stand together against our common foe.

"The Black Dragon."

A few hours later the preparations for battle were well under way. To Bobby's utter amazement, none of the villagers had packed up their things and fled into the surrounding countryside. All had decided to remain where they were and fight.

"It appears that you truly inspired them," observed the gruff voice of Cutter as he came and stood next to the teenage boy.

Bobby looked up from the dry, brittle bracken that he was packing down into the ground. "I just hope it was the right thing to do."

The creature in the form of an old man grunted to himself and nodded. "Only time will tell."

Time. Bobby shuddered at that word. The Abyss claimed to have mastery and knowledge of time. She had stated that he would go back in time to save this Sam Spallucci character, yet here he was preparing for battle.

A battle which would inevitably cause the death of numerous people.

All around him, those same people were busying themselves with their allotted tasks.

Which ones would live?

Which ones would fall to the lance?

It was impossible to tell.

Bobby shook his head. "I shouldn't be doing this," he muttered. "*Why* am I doing this?"

A steadying hand gripped his shoulder. "Because someone has to." Cutter paused before continuing. "You were right, Kanor's greatest weapon is humanity's own divisions. That's how he was able to rise so quickly and eradicate them. Sure, a sleeper army of murderous constructs lying in wait certainly helped, but if humans had been more cohesive then they could have worked together better to fight the new enemy." He gestured to the digging and labouring fugitives. "Look at them now. They are united. They at least stand a modicum of a chance. Far more than when they were arguing amongst themselves. They even have a leader."

Bobby and Cutter watched silently as Martha went from worker to worker, making sure that everyone was well and understood their allotted tasks.

After a while, Bobby turned to face his companion. "Were you there? On the day that Kanor rose?"

Cutter shook his head. "No. I and the Shadow Wraiths that followed me came much later: when the Black Dragon realised that he needed generals to martial his foot soldiers. I've been told what it was like, though, by the Black Dragon himself."

"You've actually seen Kanor?"

"Of course I have. He created me. Remember, I was the first Shadow Wraith. The rest may have been constructed by Asmodeus, but Kanor used me as a blueprint.

Bobby frowned. "Is that why you're different?"

"You mean, is that why I have a conscience?" Cutter shrugged. "I don't know. I just know that there are so many things I have done that I cannot bear the guilt of anymore. I have to do what is right. I have to help you overthrow Kanor."

Bobby studied the Wraith's old, haggard features. He allowed his eyes to travel over the creases and furrows that covered the face of the monster that had murdered his father. He took in the grey hair that was knotted and unkempt and the lips that were dry and chapped. They settled upon the grey eyes that, in return, were studying him. For a moment, construct and boy stood there in silence, simply staring intently at each other.

"Excuse me..." the voice of Martha broke the awkward moment. "Could one of you possibly check on something for us?"

Cutter nodded and, in doing so, broke eye contact with the boy that he had orphaned. "Certainly," he said. "Are you following my instructions precisely?"

The woman nodded in reply.

"I don't need to remind you that constructs are relentless. The firetrap we're setting here needs to be very wide. Even when it catches fire, they'll keep on coming."

Martha nodded once again.

"Good. I'll give it a look over." With that, he hobbled over to a ditch that the woman and her companions had been digging.

Then, as the Shadow Wraith and the female human peered down into the freshly dug earth, they froze.

Bobby frowned and cast his eyes around him. Everyone was motionless, captured in what they were doing. Some were pushing down on spades, others were lifting dry bracken into ditches. Whatever they had been doing at that precise moment had become a fresco illustrating their preparations for battle.

"Why are you wasting your time doing this?"

Bobby sighed and turned to face the girl as she became a woman.

"You will fail," said the woman.

"This is pointless," said the crone.

"You said that I was a paradox," snapped Bobby, jabbing an angry finger at the Abyss, "something that shouldn't exist in time yet does. Well, I choose to make an event that is the same as me. You say that I will fail, yet I believe that I can triumph."

The girl cocked her head thoughtfully. "No you don't."

"You believe you will fail," said the woman.

"You know that many will die," stated the crone.

Bobby tore his eyes away from the transforming entity and looked around the field of preparations. So many people. So many were depending upon him.

"You could walk away right now," suggested the girl.

"Go and do what needs to be done," said the woman.

"Save Spallucci," urged the crone.

The teenage orphan rubbed the heel of his hand against a wet tear duct. "Why is he so important to you?" he forced out. "What does he do?"

"If you save Spallucci," began the girl.

"There will be no Divergence," continued the woman.

"And Kanor will not rise," finished the crone.

"But none of these people will have ever existed!" shouted the boy, his frustration finally exploding from him. "These people are a product of the Divergent Lands. If the Divergence never happens, then I will have ripped them out of existence. At least going into battle they stand a chance of surviving."

"Do you really believe that?"

And, once more, the field was full of the sounds of activity, of humans preparing to battle against overwhelming odds in order to survive.

Bobby hung his head and refused to cry.

Chapter Four

The plan, as it stood, was quite simple. They were to lure the constructs in to engage them, then set fire to the buried bracken in the firetrap. For most of the day, the group of villagers had been following the precise instructions of Cutter concerning the digging of wide trenches in a narrow valley between two rises. He had then sent them to scavenge from the local environs all manner of dry material that they could find. This had then been packed into the earthworks. When they were finished, the trenches were full of dry bracken and scrappy pieces of wood: fuel that would ignite quickly and produce intense heat in an attempt to bake the constructs solid.

The hardest part of the excavation had

been digging up the inclines of the low hill-sides, ensuring that, when the material was ignited, it would form an effective enclosure, trapping the constructs in a kill zone.

As Bobby stared down from one of the hills at the deathtrap, he felt his stomach knotting inside of him. Below, as the light began to fade, villagers were lighting homemade torches, readying themselves to set fire to the dry material as soon as they needed to.

"It's impressive," Cutter slowly stroked his stubbled chin as he stood next to the teenage commander. "You've certainly united them."

"It's your tactical advice that has guided them."

"But…?"

"But, is it enough?"

"You doubt my plan?"

Bobby ran his fingers through his sweat-soaked hair. "Of course I do! We're taking on a whole cohort of constructs with a pile of kindling! What could possibly go wrong?"

Cutter shrugged. "A lot of things, naturally. But the alternative is for these good people to keep on running until exhaustion overcomes them and they simply lay down to die. At least, this way, they have a fighting chance."

Bobby opened his mouth to reply, but his response was cut short as an excited shout rose from below.

"They're coming! They're coming!"

Bobby and Cutter turned their heads and, from their vantage point, watched as a lone male villager ran frantically from the south. He darted across the deathtrap, his arms waving above his head.

"Where are the others?" Cutter growled. "Three went out to lure the constructs in this direction."

Bobby frowned but was immediately distracted by an all-too-familiar beat that pursued the lone villager.

Thud, thud…

Thud, thud…

Thud, thud…

The cohort of constructs rounded the base of the opposite hill. They marched as one: relentless, driven, unstoppable. Their feet rose and fell in perfect unison, each step solid and precise. They only paused when they reached the mouth of the valley. As they faced the villagers who stood before them, the constructs changed formation. They moved from their usual two-abreast phalanx and spread out to fill the entire width of the valley, creating an impassable row of three deep. As one, their arms transformed into deadly lances then together they marched on into the valley.

Slowly, carefully, the villager acting as bait edged backwards. It had been emphasised to him that his role in the charade was crucial. If he ran back too fast then the constructs might pick up speed and overshoot the killing zone. Too slow and he would be trapped with the golems when all hell broke loose.

As it was, the man played his role perfectly.

As he emerged from the firetrap, the wide band of constructs was situated perfectly in its middle.

"Now!" Bobby screamed from his spot on the hillside.

As the constructs marched as one, so the villagers responded in unison. Dipping prepared arrowheads into the flaming torches, they lifted up their hunting bows and let the fiery projectiles fly into the midst of the oncoming army. The arrows struck home and the bracken and dry wood caught the first time. Flames roared up from the ground, enveloping the constructs.

"More!" Bobby yelled. "More!"

The villagers were only happy to oblige. Bows which were more accustomed to firing on rabbits caused arrow after arrow to rain down upon new targets. More and more of the valley erupted into fire. It became a Hell on Earth, a veritable infernal pit with the creatures of clay standing in its midst. Bobby could feel the heat from the fire searing the hair on his arms as he peered down into the inferno. What he saw made his heartbeat quicken.

The constructs were standing there, baked solid. They were now immobile, a long wall of clay from one side of the valley to the other.

He gaped through a beaming grin. It

had worked! Not only that, but it had worked so quickly and without the loss of one single life.

"We did it!" Bobby gasped. "We beat them!" he turned to Cutter and paused in his jubilation. The old man was thoughtfully stroking his stubbly chin as he peered down at his hard-baked kindred. "What? What's the matter?"

The Shadow Wraith's eyes were now following the procession of villagers as they swarmed down the hillside towards their brave friend who had acted as bait. Backs were being slapped and cheers were going up as celebrations were had.

"They just stopped in the middle of the valley. Why didn't they keep marching forward?" Horror spread across the old man's face. "Get them out of there," he growled. "Now!"

But it was too late.

Thud, thud…

Thud, thud…

Thud, thud…

The celebrations petered out as the villagers turned to face the northern end of the valley. Through the rising smoke, they could make out a large, wide force of constructs advancing towards them. At their head rode not just one or two, but six Shadow Wraiths.

Panic overcame the humans and they searched for a means of escape from the oncoming assault. Their way back was blocked by the impenetrable wall of clay lances and fire. This meant that the only way out was up. Screaming, they began to clamber up the hillside opposite from Bobby and Cutter, only to be faced with a descending row of lances.

It was then that the sound of death began to fill the valley.

The first to fall were those who were highest up the hill. As was their wont, the constructs struck methodically and without mercy. Limp bodies were thrown down onto those below, causing the panicked villagers further down the slope to stumble and fall. These were then easily picked off by the advancing troops who marched solidly over their fresh corpses. The row of constructs advancing down into the valley now came into play. They surrounded the remaining villagers and, with the Shadow Wraiths harrying them from atop their mounts, they pushed them to their ultimate goal: the flaming wall of fire and lances.

Bobby could stand to watch helplessly no more. Ignoring Cutter's protests, he leapt and bounded down the hillside, reaching the fiery deathtrap before he even took a breath. Ignoring the screams of death, he grabbed a relatively larger piece of old timber from the flames and charged into the battle, furiously swinging the fiery end at anything that got in his way. In front of him, he saw Martha slump to her knees as a construct rammed its lance through her chest. Bobby charged the golem and struck it with the fiery wood. The construct simply rose from its grisly task and turned towards Bobby before advancing. The teenager watched the lance rise up level with his face and transform into a club.

Bobby was vaguely aware of the sound of running behind him before the club swung down upon his head and everything turned black.

Chapter Five

"Hello, Son."

Bobby opened his eyes. The world was at the wrong angle. The small part of it that he could see, anyway. Pushing himself up to a sitting position, the world righted itself.

Sort of.

It was level now but it was still very, very wrong.

From his seat on a wooden sofa that was covered in homemade cushions and blankets, Bobby gazed around the small, homely living room where he had awoken. The hearth roared, producing a soothing heat. Apples lay in a smoothly polished wooden bowl upon a small, finely crafted table. A woven rug, the patterns of which he remembered tracing with his infant finger, lay on the otherwise bare wooden floor.

His father sat in a chair opposite, smiling gently at him.

Bobby frowned. The last thing that he remembered…

He ran his hand tentatively across his scalp. No blood, no bone, no damage.

"Am I dead?"

His father smiled in amusement and shook his head.

"Then what is this?"

Howard's brown eyes held his son. "I can't say that I'm entirely sure, Bobby."

"Are you real?"

"As real as you need me to be, I guess." The long-dead woodworker rose from the chair he had fashioned shortly after Bobby had been born and crossed the small living room to sit on the sofa next to his son. He slipped his arm around the teenager, drew him in close and waited.

He didn't have to wait long.

Bobby began to cry. "It's so hard without you, Dad. So hard."

"I know. I know."

"Every day's a struggle. No matter what

I do, life just seems to get harder and harder. So many people have died. Innocent people. I can't stop it."

"You're just a boy," came the soft voice of the adult. "How can you *expect* to stop it?"

"But someone has to! This can't go on forever. It's not right!"

"And why does it have to be you?"

Bobby sat cradled in his father's arms, tears tracking down his cheeks. "Whichever way I turn, it's always there, confronting me. I can't escape it. If I turn my back on it, it just walks around and stands before me once again.

"I'm so tired."

"I know, Son. I know."

"And Katy…"

Bobby felt the spirit of his father sigh beside his cheek.

"I failed."

Howard drew back and, placing his workman's hands on his son's shoulders, looked the lad straight in the eye. "Now, that is far from the truth."

"But, she left me. She ran away to be with Asherah."

"And why should the actions of your sister be your fault?"

"I drove her away! She left because she was cross with me."

"No. Katy did what she did because of something far darker."

The image of the older and vampiric version of his sister rose up in Bobby's mind. "What's wrong with her?"

"I don't know, Bobby. I truly don't. But, whatever demons Katy is fighting, they are not of your doing." Howard ran his callused fingers through his son's dark mop of hair. "She has always been strong-willed, defiant. So opposite to your kindly nature. She needs to find her own path. She needs someone to teach her how to control the raging tempest inside of her."

"But, Asherah…?"

Howard's head rocked from side to side. "Do not dismiss the Fallen offhand. She is a somewhat complex being."

Bobby frowned. "If you say so, I guess." He looked up at his father's kind face, one he hadn't seen for so many years. "It's good to see you."

"And you," his father smiled, before a more serious demeanour swept across him. "So, what are you going to do now?"

"What do you mean?"

"Well, in a moment, you're going to wake up, with an awful headache, I might add, and you're going to be faced with a choice. What will your answer be?"

Bobby nodded. "Should I go to Wellington? Should I travel back in time and save Sam Spallucci?"

Howard returned the nod.

Bobby ran his fingers through his hair. "I don't trust the Abyss," he said. "There's something… *slippery* about her. She feels like a prize fish you might see basking in the summer sun at the bottom of a clear brook. You creep up on it, carefully keeping out of the sunlight so as to not scare it with your shadow. Then, slowly, so slowly, you slip your hands, fingers outspread, under its belly and you grasp it, only to feel it slide effortlessly out of your grip. Yes, she's just like that fish. She is what she is. She's not pretending to be anything that she isn't, but she knows so much more than I do, just as the fish knows that it is safe from my grasping fingers. I could kneel by that small brook all day and never manage to get a hold of the fish; I could spend my entire life trying to fathom what the Abyss is up to, what she really wants, and never form a coherent answer."

"You could walk away."

Bobby's head sank down to his chest. "I know. Like you said, I'm just a boy."

"And how would that make you feel?"

"As rotten as the last apple in the barrel."

Howard smiled. "Humanity is a very precious thing, Son. It is like a fine cloth that has been woven and then embroidered with an intricate pattern. However, someone is teasing at a loose thread, unravelling all the time and effort that its creator has spent on it. If they continue to pull then, one day, there will be nothing left."

"But how can I be the one to put things right?"

"Perhaps it's not your job to do so? Perhaps this Spallucci chap is a dab hand with a darning needle?"

"And in saving him, I save humanity?" Bobby pondered this for a moment. "But if he prevents the Divergence, what about everyone who has lived since Kanor rose?"

"Do you really think they've had lives worth living? Perhaps they will be born into new lives. Better lives?"

"I hadn't thought of that." Bobby rested his head against his father's chest once again. "I miss you."

"And I miss you too. But I'll always be with you."

Bobby nodded. "In my thoughts and my dreams."

"Exactly. Walk well and stay safe, Bobby."

"Walk well and stay safe, Dad."

With that, the teenage boy allowed his eyes to slide shut.

Bobby opened his eyes for the second time and winced. His father had been correct. He had a hell of a headache.

Rather than lying on a long chair in his childhood home, he found himself lying on a soft patch of ground, the grass moulded to his face. Carefully, he pushed himself up and, after the world had stopped swaying, took in his immediate surroundings. In front of him was a roaring campfire. Its heat was welcome as the night had drawn in and the stars looked down from a clear sky. Without the dancing flames, Bobby would have been chilled to the core.

He was not alone by the fire. There were two others, both familiar.

On his left, bound tightly across his chest by what appeared to be a piece of rope, knelt the sole surviving member of the group of villagers that had gone out to lure in the construct cohort. The man's clothing was ragged and torn and his face was a patchwork of bruises.

But that was not all.

As Bobby studied the purple marks on the wretch's face, he saw blood trickling down from the man's closed eyelids. Bobby moved closer to study him and the man flinched. His head snapped back and forth with his eyelids still shut. "Who's there?" he called out. "Please! Please!"

"Quiet down," came a rough voice from

the other side of the fire, "or I'll take your tongue as well as your eyes."

The villager slumped nervously back into his former position and Bobby turned his attention to Cutter.

The old man was tending to something on the fire. "How are you doing?" he asked.

"Better than," Bobby motioned towards the blind villager, "him, apparently. What did you do?"

Without taking his eyes off what he was tending to on the campfire, Cutter replied, "Well, first I rescued you from the construct that had just bludgeoned you unconscious. Then I grabbed our guest over there and brought us to this place which is quite safe… for now. As you slept, I had a chat with our friend about loyalty and what would make a man throw it away as if it were a warm pot of piss. Then…" He pulled a stick out of the fire and the aroma of cooked rabbit caused Bobby's stomach to growl. "I cooked you some food." He offered the meat across to the teenage boy.

Bobby nodded and took the meal. "Thank you," he said before devouring the tasty morsels. "How long was I unconscious?"

"Most of the night." Cutter rummaged in his pocket and drew out a pouch from which he emptied some smoking material into his pipe. Taking another stick from the fire, he lit the bowl and inhaled deeply. The aromatic fragrance of the mixture mingled pleasantly with that of the cooked rabbit. "How are you feeling?"

Bobby finished the meat and glanced across at the prisoner. "Cautious," he replied. "Why? Why did you do that to him?"

The old man drew heavily on his pipe and regarded the prisoner on the other side of the campfire. "I needed answers."

"But, blinding him?"

"Bobby, that wretch sold out his entire village. It was he who was the original informant and then told the force of constructs that were pursuing us about our ambush. He watched as the rest of his team were put to the lance. He did nothing. He then led the constructs back to us and stood by as everyone else was massacred.

"And do you know why he did all this?"

Bobby shook his head.

"Tell the boy your grand reason," Cutter called across the fire. "Tell him why you sold out your friends."

The man's shoulders rose and fell. His head jerked from side to side.

"Do you want me to come over there and resume our little chat?"

The man's head shook more violently.

"Then spill your story."

"They… they said I was useless. They said that I was no good at my job."

"Which was…?"

The man mumbled something unintelligible.

"We didn't hear you. Why don't I come and get your tongue and it can whisper in our ears after I've cut it from your mouth?"

"I emptied their cesspits. They said I didn't do a thorough enough job."

"So, you betrayed them all and let the constructs slaughter everyone."

"No! No! Please. It wasn't like that. I didn't betray them."

Cutter rolled his eyes, dragged himself up from his spot by the fire and stamped over to the prisoner. "Here we go again. Really? You're still claiming this was all a big misunderstanding? Tell me then, just how did you escape when the others died?"

"I ran. I just ran. The mud buckets let me go."

"They let you go?"

"Yeah. I got a head start and they followed me as per the plan."

"Really?"

"That's right."

"The thing is, if a construct has you at the end of its lance, it won't hesitate to kill you. They let you go because you told them about the trap. You betrayed your friends and family."

"That's crazy! Why would I do that and, anyway, how would you know what a construct would do?"

Bobby's hands flew to his mouth as Cutter's arm shot out far longer than humanly possible, a sharp point at its end, and thrust through the chest of the blind prisoner.

"You'd be surprised..." Cutter murmured as the dying man twitched and spasmed on the lance.

When he was sure that the man was dead, Cutter withdrew his arm and took a deep draw from his pipe before blowing a long stream of smoke through his pursed lips. "So there you have it. The guy who shovels shit had a chip on his shoulder after a bit of criticism and decided that the correct response would be to have the rest of his village slaughtered." He turned to Bobby. "And people call *me* a monster."

Bobby sat silently, his eyes fixed on the slumped, bleeding corpse.

"I've been on this rock a good number of years now, Bobby. It's the same all over. People... *humans*... are selfish. They look out for number one. They do whatever they can to better themselves. They will trample over the fresh corpses of children should it mean they have a better life."

Bobby shook his head. "No. That's not true. It's not humans. It's this world. It's the Divergent Lands. It's what Kanor did to them that makes them do awful things like..." he pointed to the corpse, "he did."

Cutter raised an eyebrow. "Really? So

it was all pansies and puppies before the Black Dragon rose, then? There was no war, no poverty, no jealousy, no hatred?"

"Well, yes, there was, but that was due to…"

"To what? People treating other people like the muck this vermin was supposed to shovel?" Cutter chuckled darkly and refilled his pipe. "Yes Bobby, Kanor has done terrible things. I should know. I've done them for him. But it was no different before his rise. Humanity is a perverse, corrupt monster that rose from the ground and devoured all that stood before it, before turning on itself. Did you know that they had weapons that could have obliterated the entire planet? The entire planet, Bobby! Kanor may have decimated them, but humanity could have wiped its own entire species from the face of the Earth. They even tried a few times. Once, they desolated nearly a whole country. Millions dead in the blink of an eye!"

"Just like your kind did on the day of the Divergence?"

"But, we had no choice. We were created that way. We were the weapons, not the one wielding them. Humanity…" The Shadow Wraith shook his head. "They were innocent at some point, I guess. But, somewhere along the way, someone gave them a nice, long pointy stick and showed them which end was safer to hold whilst jabbing it into their neighbour."

Bobby pondered this. "But, if that's the case, then surely, it's still not their fault. Someone corrupted them."

"Maybe," Cutter shrugged. "Maybe they just decided that the sound of screaming was a beautiful melody to which they could rock their dying babies to sleep at night. What can you do about it? Go back and find the exact point in time that a human first picked up a rock and caved in the brains of his brother?"

"No, but I can stop all," he waved his hands around him, "*this* from happening. I can give humanity a second chance to get things right."

Cutter's eyes narrowed and his dark pupils twinkled in the firelight.

"And just how do you think you could

achieve such a momentous task?"

Chapter Six

"This is a terrible plan."

As Bobby stood at the edge of the wide lake that surrounded the towering edifice of All Saints church, there was a distinctly large part of him that agreed with Cutter's succinct appraisal of their current situation.

It had taken a few days to travel from their previous location, even with the Shadow Wraith transformed into the shape of a strong black stallion. This had given the equine simulacrum plenty of opportunity to voice his opinion on the task at hand.

His first bone of contention had been the trustworthiness of the Abyss. "How can you believe anything that she tells you?" the horse had demanded. "She is a timeless ocean that encircles reality. What would it serve her to dabble in human affairs?"

"But, you could ask the opposite, couldn't you?" Bobby had replied. "She has no personal need to interfere. Like you said, she is a being outside of our…" He sought in vain for the correct word, eventually just waving his hand around them at the barren land across which they travelled. "…all this. So, perhaps she's just being benevolent? Perhaps she is looking with pity on the mere mortals that she sees suffering through time?"

"Perhaps," Cutter had grumbled. "Perhaps she is just using you?"

"To what end? As you said, she is an ocean that surrounds our Realm. Whatever could she want?"

The second point that Cutter raised was regarding the man that Bobby was supposed to save. "Why Spallucci? You know nothing of the guy."

"Claw held him in high esteem."

This had provoked a harsh snort from the horse's nostrils and an annoyed stamping of its hooves. "Seriously? You buy into this *Man of Virtue* garbage? No. It's a fallacy. There is no such person."

"Not if he's already dead. What if I went back and saved Spallucci and he turned out to be the Virtuous Man? What if he's destined to stop the rise of Kanor? What if that's the Man of Virtue's role in all of this?"

"I don't like that many *what ifs...*"

"But it could be a chance for us to stop all this horror from ever occurring."

"And how do you expect to find him? The world is a very large place."

"She said that she would transport me directly to Lancaster, the city where he lives. It shouldn't be too hard to find him there, I would imagine."

"Towns were much bigger back then, Bobby. I'm not sure you really know what it is that you're letting yourself in for."

"But I have to try," the boy had said. "If I don't, who will?"

So, in due time, they had arrived at Wellington. Bobby had dismounted at the edge of the town and Cutter had resumed his old man form. "I am guessing that I do not have to say that we need to exercise the utmost caution here," he had warned.

It had been like walking through a town that had died. The crumbling buildings were decaying bones; broken glass was rotten flesh. Not a sound resonated through the place, not even the breath of the slightest breeze. Everything was still, inert. Bobby had thought that the place would be swarming with constructs, but this was not the case. The two of them made their way through the ghost town unimpeded until, finally, they found themselves on the side of a vast lake that surrounded the old church.

Bobby looked up at his companion. "What now? How do we cross?"

"On that." Cutter raised a gnarled finger and gestured to a figure looming out of a misty gloom that hung over the glasslike surface of the lake. The sound of water lapping against wood and the creaking of rusted metal reached the teenager's ears as he witnessed a ghastly figure emerge into view. Slowly, with no apparent need to hurry his task at hand, a man used a long pole to push a thin boat towards them. Dressed in tattered rags, the ferryman was tall and gaunt. A dark cowl covered most of his head, but Bobby could just about make out a face of long, drawn features that possessed a pair of milky eyes.

The boat eventually bumped up against the stony shoreline and Cutter climbed aboard as Bobby tentatively followed.

The ferryman held out a pale withered hand, making a grasping motion with his bony fingers.

"There's no need for that." Cutter's voice was low and menacing.

The ferryman struck his hand out once more.

"What does he want?" Bobby asked.

"Payment."

"Surely we have goods that we can give him?" Bobby took his pack from his back and made to open it in order to look inside for something suitable.

Cutter placed a hand on the boy's shoulder. "Trust me. You are no longer in possession of the payment that this being requires. You handed it to someone else quite a while back."

Bobby frowned as he tried to work out

what the old man meant before realisation dawned on his face. "The Eternal Talisman! Its purpose was to see the Virtuous Man across the lake? But how can we cross?"

"Simple," Cutter smiled as his skin began to ripple. "I pull rank." He pulled himself up straight and there, in the boat, stood his true form. That of a Shadow Wraith.

The ferryman leaned forward and peered closely at the construct with his milky eyes. Then, nodding in acceptance, he thrust the long pole into the water and pushed them away from the shoreline. Cutter grunted in apparent satisfaction and transformed back into his usual shape.

The journey across the lake was a short one and it was in no time at all that the barge thumped to a halt. The silent ferryman stood passively as his passengers disembarked. Then, when his services were no longer required, he pushed the boat back out into the mist.

"No going back now," Cutter mused, rubbing an arthritic hand against his stubbled chin. He turned and gazed up at the old church. "I haven't been here for a very long time. It hasn't changed." He took a deep breath and made for what appeared to be the entrance. Bobby followed him up into a stone porchway. Before them stood the remains of an old wooden door. The material of the door looked like it was black but it was rotten and its scant remains were covered in mildew.

Bobby wrinkled his nose. "The rot makes it smell sour."

Cutter grunted. "That's not just the stench of decay. It's an odour of something far more unpleasant. Magic." He approached the remains of the rotten door. "Shall we?"

In the pit of his stomach, Bobby felt the swelling waves of a sea of nausea but, in his head, there was nothing but clarity. This was where he was meant to be. Everything over the last few weeks had led him to this place. Every single step, every action, had brought him to stand here upon the threshold of the lair of the Black Dragon.

He had a job to do and do it he would.

Bobby nodded and stepped past Cutter into the old church.

The inside of the ancient building was everything that Bobby had expected. The first thing that struck him was the rise tenfold of the foetid stench. He found himself retching and holding a fist to his mouth as he controlled his body's reflexive reaction to the foul odour. When he had brought his gagging under control, he looked around and decided that, before Kanor had chosen it as his dwelling place, the church would have been a place of beauty. Large windows reached to the roof. Long ago, they would have allowed sunlight to stream through on the worshippers, bathing them in a rainbow of colours from what looked like stained glass. Now, though, the glass was mostly shattered and the roof itself was ripped apart above where Bobby and Cutter were standing.

Bobby cast his eyes around into the gloom of the dead building. On his right, a long screen seemed to traverse the main body of the church, passing under gigantic stone arches. Atop it was a decayed figure of a man on what appeared to be a cross, his arms spread out wide and nailed to the wood. At first, Bobby winced, thinking it was some sort of victim of the Black Dragon, but then he realised that it was a wooden carving. Breathing out in relief, he looked down the other end of the building, to his extreme left.

And there he saw the font.

Tapping Cutter on the arm, he made to step towards the stone bowl, but the old man's hand shot out and grabbed him by the wrist. Bobby turned and frowned at his companion, but then followed his eyes into the darkness on the opposite side of the church.

There was movement.

To begin with, it was just the hint of a shadow but then the movement took form and stalked out of the darkness, taking the shape of not just one construct but many. Bobby felt his guts lurch as he heard the sound of transformation next to him. Glancing quickly at Cutter, he saw that the man's arms were now a pair of deadly lances.

"Run!" Cutter barked. "Go for the font!" and he sprung into the middle of the church to confront his kindred.

Bobby needed no repetition of the command and his feet pounded beneath him as he darted to his left. His ears were aware of the sound of fighting but his eyes were focused on his goal, the stone bowl at the back of the church. He leapt over old wooden seats and ducked under fallen beams as he homed in on his target. A loud cry came from his right but he ignored it. He knew that there was nothing he could do to help his friend. He had one task and one task alone.

He had to reach the font.

And he almost did.

He was just crossing a clear patch of flooring when a loose flagstone rocked under his foot and his ankle twisted. Screaming out in pain, Bobby fell to the floor, the stone flags cracking against his knee. He rolled to his feet, making to lunge for the font, but there was a terrifyingly familiar wet sound behind him and he cried out as an extended clay limb wrapped around the wrist of his outstretched hand. He felt himself pulled sharply around and was face to eyeless face with a gigantic construct that towered above him.

Bobby was transported back many years to that day when he had first encountered one of these mud buckets, back in the village square of Irlingbury. He remembered how the rest of the villagers had been terrified, how they had held their breath as the monster had loomed over the small boy.

As the construct in front of him raised its lance, Bobby now found himself doing as those villagers did all those years ago. The eyeless beast opened its wide gash of a mouth and its dark tongue slipped out from between its clay lips. The tongue snaked to and fro as it scented the air between itself and its captive. The raised lance paused mid-air.

A demonic roar exploded behind the construct and its lance fell, dismembered, to the floor.

The golem staggered around to face its attacker and was presented with a sharp scythe that cleft it straight down the middle. Both halves of the monster slipped silently to the ground to reveal a battered and frantic

Cutter.

As Bobby crawled to his feet, pushing the lifeless arm from his wrist, he winced at the sight of a wide hole gaping through the old man's shoulder. Cutter's eyes followed those of the boy and he shuddered as the wound miraculously closed shut.

"Now," the Shadow Wraith that had saved his life said, "while there is still time."

Bobby nodded and turned towards the font.

As his hand reached out, the sound of someone clapping reached his ears.

He paused and turned around. There, walking down the middle of the church was a robed figure. It wore a dark cloak, the cowl of which obscured its face. Carefully, it sidestepped the pools of clay that Cutter had left in his wake.

"Marvellous!" came the dry male voice. "Absolutely marvellous! Such a fine show. I haven't seen the like in many, many years."

Cutter stepped in front of Bobby, shielding the boy. "Leave him be."

The robed figure stopped, slid his hands into his sleeves and appeared to cock his head in thought. "Now why would I ever harm the boy?"

"You just set your constructs on him!"

"Did I?" The cowl appeared to study the wet pools of clay that were disturbingly edging themselves away into the shadows of the church. "Did any of them actually harm him? I think not." He walked up to Cutter and said, "You really are so suspicious, you know. Mind you, that was to be expected, I guess."

Bobby could just make out a touch of a smile in the shadows of the cowl as it turned to face him.

"Hello, Bobby," came the voice. "Please allow me to introduce myself. I'm Kanor. But then, I'm guessing you've already worked that out. You are such a bright lad, after all."

Bobby swallowed his nerves and forced his tongue and lips to move. "What… what do you want?"

"Why, peace of course. Just like everyone else. It's just that, you know, I achieved it. So, there you go. Good for me!"

Bobby pushed past his protector.

"Peace! Peace? You call all this peace? Seriously?"

"How else should I describe it, Bobby," Kanor shrugged. "Tell me, when was the last time you saw a war? When was the last time you heard of humans taking up arms against each other? Never! That's when. And you have me to thank for it.

"I united humanity. I thinned the herd. There were so many of them. Far too many, in fact. All with their different beliefs and cultures. All with their own differing opinions on how to move forward. You know, many years ago, someone once said to me that humanity, as a species, doesn't do different. So, I made it all the same.

"In doing so, I brought peace."

"But… you slaughtered billions!"

Kanor gave another shrug. "What can I say, a difficult nut needs a large hammer with which to crack open its shell."

Bobby shook his head and felt his feet turn beneath him. He felt himself spin around, leaving the crazed ruler of a dead world behind him. One foot slapped down on the stone floor in front of another as they propelled him towards the font. He watched his arm, reaching out under the command of sheer rational thought and emotion, touch the rim of the font...

And suddenly he was somewhere else entirely.

Epilogue

The Shadow Wraith stood before his maker. The question that went through the created being's mind was, "What now?"

The hooded figure turned his back on his creation.

Cutter lifted his arm. It was still in the shape of a scythe, the deadly weapon with which the monster in front of him had blessed him. He could use it now. One swift strike would dispatch the being who had caused the deaths and suffering of billions.

He lifted his arm and took a purposeful step forward.

Then stopped, immobile in his tracks.

He pushed with all his might against his arm, willing it to sweep down and cleave his creator in two. But the limb remained motionless.

Kanor paused. His cowl moved slightly before he nodded and turned towards the font. "Well?"

A column of water rose from the depths of the stone bowl. The Black Dragon stood patiently before it as the swirling liquid took the form of a girl, then a woman, then a crone before gracefully stepping down onto the stone floor. As its foot touched the ground, the same flagstone that had only recently caused a teenage boy to stumble rocked under the weight of the fluid entity.

A small smile touched the lips of the ever-changing face of the Abyss.

"It is done," said Kanor.

"I know," said the girl.

"Of course you do. You know everything. Even how you were supposed to die."

"…and there will be no more Sea…" mused the woman.

Deep within his hood, the Black Dragon grunted.

"You seem… *conflicted*," observed the crone as she walked slowly around humanity's decimator.

"Will this work?"

The girl paused in front of the cowled figure. "What an odd question, you ask."

"You know it will," stated the woman.

Kanor approached the font that bore the acrostic of his name. "That's not what I mean. I mean…"

"The end of everything," the girl finished.

"I've sacrificed so much because of it."

The woman: "You have done what had to be done."

The crone: "And there is more still to be done."

Kanor nodded and traced a finger along the words that were engraved along the edge of the font. "My army is ready. It is time to start sending them back through time; time to sow the seeds of my rising. You can definitely do this?"

"The blood spell was broken when the battle was fought in this place," explained the girl.

Kanor nodded. "The day of the event in Israel. I remember it well."

"As you should," said the woman.

"It was the day that Sam Spallucci died at your hands," finished the crone.

A dry chuckle emanated from the dark cowl. "Indeed it was. Indeed it was." Kanor turned to face the figure of Cutter who still stood with his scythe arm outstretched above his head. "So, we had better begin. This one first, I think. I have a very special job for him."

"I'll never serve you again," Cutter growled, tugging defiantly at his immobile limb. "I broke your hold over me."

Raucous laughter filled the church. "Oh, God. That's so funny. It really is." Wiping tears of laughter away from his shadowed eyes, Kanor came nose to nose with his creation. "I really did do a good job on you, didn't I?"

Confusion swept across the Wraith's face.

"Don't worry. In a few seconds, all will become clear." Then, leaning forward and whispering in the construct's ear, a solitary word left Kanor's lips, "Chimera," before he took a calm step backwards.

Cutter's mouth formed a round O shape and he stared up at his outstretched limb. Shaking his head, he transformed it back into an arm and, flexing his fingers, he sank down in reverence onto one knee.

"What is my master's bidding?"

Bobby Normal will return in
Sam Spallucci: Lux Æterna

Author's Notes

Well, there you have it, the climax of my five-book Bobby Normal series. Did it end how you thought it would when you started reading it back in *Bobby Normal and the Eternal Talisman*? I have to say, the scene of Bobby in All Saints was just a distant impression in my own head, way back in 2017.

Bobby started out as a little side distraction for me. As I mentioned in the Author's Notes for *Bobby Normal and the Eternal Talisman*, I was working on *Sam Spallucci: Dark Justice,* more specifically the scene where Sam first encounters a construct in all its clay-based glory, when I started to wonder what the foot soldiers of Kanor would look like to a child. I was also considering back then what the world would be like post-Divergence. I started to sketch out a world that I had been planning since I was a teenager and, out of this melting pot, Bobby was born.

Over the subsequent years, the first book was reshaped and remoulded until I felt it "worked". I, personally, have never really been a fan of the Young Adult genre. Even as a teenager I felt that it has a tendency to oversimplify matters at the expense of the plot. So, as I toiled over *Eternal Talisman*, I made sure that my own outing still possessed my style and voice, ensuring that I did not patronise readers young and old, leaving hidden nuggets for them to discover on their journey through the Divergent Lands. This feeling has carried on throughout the series and indeed it has developed just as Katy and Bobby have developed in this terrifying world in which they live, both now walking their own paths.

I think it was whilst I was starting on *Bobby Normal and the Virtuous Man* that the idea of Bobby crossing over into Sam's world was starting to prickle away at the back of my head. He and Sam are both similar individuals: thrust into this supernatural world that is beyond their control; lost their fathers at early ages; pulled left and right by individuals who know more than they let on. It became inevitable that they would eventually cross paths. I actually wrote *Sam Spallucci: Lux Æterna* before *Black Dragon*. However, I have delayed its publication so that it would fit more consistently with the Bobby Normal story flow, so to speak. I won't say too much here because, you know, spoilers but, as the end of this book states, Bobby will return, albeit briefly, in Sam's eighth adventure before the two of them team up in Sam's penultimate book, *Sam Spallucci: Dare The Dragon*.

There's a lot more that I could say about *Black Dragon* but it would take far too long for me to ramble on about all the little points that lead to things in the future. If you want to devour those, then I suggest you head over to my website, www.aschambers.co.uk, and follow the link to my YouTube channel. There you'll find numerous Easter Egg videos about this series and the Sam Spallucci books.

Having said that, there are just two other characters that I need to mention here. Not doing so would cause both of them a severe injustice.

First: Katy. I think Katy Normal has to be one of my personal favourite creations. Compared to Bobby, she has developed a completely different view of the cards that life has dealt her. Whereas her brother is far more stoic, she is proactive and angry. She is determined to grab life by the scruff of the neck and throttle it until it submits. At the time of writing this, Katy currently appears in two more, as yet unpublished, works. Sam crosses paths with a slightly older version of her in *Lux Æterna* and we come across her at the same time period in a short story that will be published in *Hear My Scare*, an anthology that I have planned for early 2025. We will see how seven or eight years with Asherah will have changed her and will have set her on the path to the adult that she wants to become.

And what will adult life hold for this tempestuous eight-year-old? Well, that way spoilers lie, but I think the implications in this series have been fairly obvious. I'll leave it there and we can catch up with her in the *Divergent Lands* series which should be out in about six years or so.

The second character I have to chat about, before you head back into your real-world life, is Cutter. The gnarled old man was an immediate fan favourite with my readers. When I started the series I was watching *Breaking Bad* and *Better Call Saul*. My favourite character in both series has to be Mike Ehrmantraut, played by the out-standing Jonathan Banks. Cutter is un-ashamedly based upon Banks' portrayal of this ex-cop who is dragged ever deeper into the murky world of drug cartels as he be-comes an enforcer for Gus Fring. His battered appearance and world-weary de-meanour fitted Cutter perfectly. We root for Mike just as we root for Cutter. Even when we start to see things that make us doubt his intentions, we still like him as a character. All I will say here is that you haven't seen the last of the Shadow Wraith yet.

So, anyway, there you have it. I'll stop whiffling on here and let you get back to your lives. If you would be so kind as to leave some sort of review or rating over on Amazon or Goodreads, I would be eternally grateful. You can find links on my website.

Have a great day and I'll see you next time.

Walk well and stay safe!
ASC October 2023.

Bobby Normal And The Black Dragon

About The Author

A.S.Chambers resides in Lancaster, England. He lives a fairly simple life of walking in the countryside, gazing at mountains and rescuing his cat from the net curtains.

He is quite happy for, and in fact would encourage, you to follow him on Facebook, Instagram, TikTok, YouTube, Threads and Twitter.

There is also a nice, shiny website:
www.aschambers.co.uk

www.ingramcontent.com/pod-product-compliance
Lightning Source LLC
Chambersburg PA
CBHW031252210726
48287CB00003B/1011